George Walker

A Collection of the Minute and Rare Shells

lately discovered in the sand of the sea shore near Sandwich

George Walker

A Collection of the Minute and Rare Shells
lately discovered in the sand of the sea shore near Sandwich

ISBN/EAN: 9783337392185

Printed in Europe, USA, Canada, Australia, Japan

Cover: Foto ©Andreas Hilbeck / pixelio.de

More available books at **www.hansebooks.com**

T E S T A C E A

M I N U T A   R A R I O R A,

Nuperrime detecta in Arena

L I T T O R I S   S A N D V I C E N S I S;

A GUL. BOYS, Arm. S. A. S.

Multa addidit, et omnium Figuras ope Microfcopii ampliatas accurate delineavit.

GEO. WALKER.

A   C O L L E C T I O N

OF THE

Minute and Rare S H E L L S,

LATELY DISCOVERED

In the Sand of the Sea Shore near SANDWICH;

By WILLIAM BOYS, Efq; F. S. A.

Confiderably augmented, and all their Figures accurately drawn, as magnified
with the Microfcope.

By GEO. WALKER, Bookfeller, at FAVERSHAM.

L O N D O N:
PRINTED BY J. MARCH;

And Sold by B. WHITE, in Fleet Street; Meffrs. SCATCHERD and WHITAKER, in
Ave-Maria Lane; and W. HUMPHREY, St. Martin's Lane, near Charing Crofs;
and at FAVERSHAM, by the AUTHOR.

T O

THE MOST NOBLE HER GRACE

The Dutchefs Dowager of *P O R T L A N D*;

A N D T O

Sir *J O S E P H B A N K S*, Baronet, P. R. S.

MOST ZEALOUS PROMOTERS OF EVERY LAUDABLE ATTEMPT TO INCREASE
THE KNOWLEDGE OF THE HISTORY OF NATURE;

THIS DESCRIPTION OF THE

M I N U T E A N D R A R E S H E L L S,

L A T E L Y D I S C O V E R E D

O N T H E S E A C O A S T O F S A N D W I C H,

AND OTHER ADJOINING PARTS IN THE COUNTY OF KENT:

I N T E S T I M O N Y O F

AN HEART-FELT GRATITUDE FOR THE VERY OBLIGING ATTENTION AND
GENEROSITY THEY HAVE BEEN PLEASED TO BESTOW

U P O N I T S P U B L I C A T I O N;

IS MOST HUMBLY DEDICATED

BY THEIR EVER DEVOTED, AND

MOST OBEDIENT SERVANT,

G E O. W A L K E R.

THE

INTRODUCTION.

THE firſt diſcovery of the curious minute Shells, exhibited in this collection, originates with that inquiſitive naturaliſt William Boys, Eſq; F. S. A. of Sandwich, in the county of Kent ; who, by his unremitting reſearches into the works of Nature, was happily induced to examine with his glaſſes the Sand of the adjoining ſhore, whereby he diſcovered a conſiderable number of minute Shells, altogether new to him, lodged therein.

Information of this having been communicated to my worthy friend, Edward Jacob, Eſq; F. S. A. Mr. Boys was earneſtly preſſed by him to proſecute the diſcovery, with the offer of procuring aſſiſtance in the purſuit, if his other neceſſary avocations would not permit him to employ it ſo cloſely as Mr. Jacob wiſhed : The propoſal being readily accepted by Mr. Boys, Mr. Jacob was pleaſed to make an offer of the employment to me, which I entered upon moſt willingly ; and, upon receiving ſeveral parcels of Sand from Mr. Boys, I purſued the following method in examining them :—Firſt, I placed ſmall portions of it when dry under Dr. Withering's botanical Microſcope, in order to ſeparate the Shells from the Sand, and afterwards proceeded to enlarge every ſingle Shell with the greater magnifiers of Cuff's Microſcope for opaque objects, and Wilſon's pocket one ; and by theſe aids I drew them as exhibited in the plates.

And.

And here it may not be unacceptable to inform future Inquirers that, in order to facilitate the more eafy difcovery of thefe minute objects, after the Sand was perfectly dry, I put a handful on an open fheet of paper, and gently fhook it from fide to fide, by which means, the minute Shells being lighter than the fand, were feparated from and lay above it, and were thereby much more expeditioufly procured, than by any other means I could think of. It is alfo advifeable to place the objects for infpection in a fituation where no fudden blaft of air can come, otherwife, being very light, they may be unexpectedly blown away, as I have too frequently experienced thereby the lofs of feveral rare fpecimens ; indeed a carelefs breathing or cough, while they were under examination, hath been attended with the fame difagreeable accident.

I beg leave to obferve to Gentlemen, efpecially to thofe who have read Plancus's treatife, that, although the Sand of our coaft contains fo great a variety of fpecimens, yet it is by no means fo productive as the Sand at Rimino, leaft, defpairing of fuccefs in their firft trials, they may be induced to lay afide their further inquiries ; they cannot fail however of finding fome of the moft common in every parcel of it.

The undertaking to make the enlarged drawings by the Microfcope exact, from my want of practice, and the fmallnefs of the objects, was a matter of more difficulty than I was aware of, and required much time and patience to overcome.——Perfeverance however hath enabled me to reprefent the objects, not only to the fatisfaction of my two worthy friends, Mr. Jacob and Mr. Boys, but alfo of that moft noble Lady her Grace the Dutchefs Dowager of Portland, who hath been pleafed to accept of feveral of the minute Shells here engraved, and whofe generous approbation and affiftance in this publication can never be forgotten without the higheft ingratitude. To this noble patronage I am happy to add, that of the very refpectable and con-fummate naturalift Sir Jofeph Banks, Bart. Prefident of the Royal Society, who hath condefcended, not only to compare the drawings with a confiderable

number

number of the Shells here exhibited, but also to approve, and very generously to promote the undertaking, for which singular favors I can never be sufficiently thankful.

The approbation of two such very eminent personages, I flatter myself, cannot fail to ensure a favourable reception of my endeavours from every curious admirer of the wonderful works of our benificent CREATOR! especially those of our own island, as so large a number of Shells, heretofore unknown, are hereby added to the British Conchology, sufficient to shew the path is now laid open, and made easy for still greater discoveries to be made by inquisitive naturalists, in the different parts of the kingdom. What a number of minute Shells, equal to a moiety of the engraved English series, hath now been discovered in small quantities of Sand from an inconsiderable part of our coasts! Surely this is encouragement, and will be an inducement to Gentlemen of a philosophical turn of mind occasionally to employ their leisure hours in similar researches ; nor can they fail of making discoveries that will amply repay them for their inquiries. Indeed it is somewhat surprising, that the Authors of our own country, who have so advantageously applied the Microscope to a variety of objects of the animal kingdom, should totally have neglected to examine the shores of our own seas, crouded as they are with objects, equally worthy their attention, and yet it has not been for want of hints. The account of the minute and rare Shells discovered at Rimino, on the coast of the Adriatic Sea, was published by Plancus in the year 1739 ; and Mr. Baker's observation, in page 244, of his treatise on the Microscope, published in the year 1742, deserved more attention than has been paid to it. Shell fish, says he, " Are objects that have as yet been very slightly examined by " the Microscope, and therefore the serious inquirer into Nature's secret " operations may here be certain of discovering beauties, which at present " he can have no conception of."

But thus it is, Nature opens her rich and inexhaustible treasures slowly and gradually to the inquisitive mind of man. The fact is, different observers
have

have generally different purfuits, otherwife thefe objects would fcarcely have efcaped the attention of many other Gentlemen, as well as of the quick-fighted Mr. Ellis, a juftly celebrated Author, who hath fo clearly inveftigated and defcribed the corals and corallines of the adjoining coafts.

To Mr. *B O Y S*, all praife is juftly due from every lover of natural fcience, for his happy and fuccefsful inveftigation of this part of our natural hiftory, which hath fo long continued unexplored.

Being anxious of adding ftill more to this elegant collection, than the Sand from Sandwich had afforded, I have examined the fediments of various parts of the fhores, from thence up to Faverfham, and the ifle of Shepey, as well as the banks of frefh water ftreams and ditches, the boggy places, and the woods in this neighbourhood, whereby very confiderable additions have been made, which are noticed in the explanatory index.

When the drawings were finifhed, there remained an almoft infurmountable difficulty in my properly arranging and defcribing the Shells; thro' my fmall acquaintance with Conchology, neverthelefs this was overcome, by the obliging affiftance of my antient friend Mr. Jacob, who always willing to inftruct me in my weak refearches in natural hiftory, moft kindly engaged in the tafk, tho' fo liable to cenfure.

The Claffification is agreeable to that of the greateft illuminator of natural hiftory the Sun ever fhone upon the illuftrious Linnæus however, in a retrograde courfe; as that feemed more fuitable to this collection—if the defcriptions fhould be deemed fomewhat imperfect, and not fufficiently clear, a reference may be had, for further fatisfaction, to the engravings, which may be depended upon as very exact copies of the originals, altho' fo much enlarged. Their natural fize may be known by the fmall figures at the bottom or on the fide of each enlarged fpecimen; and where there is no mark or minute figure fubjoined, that is of the real fize or notice, will be taken of the omiffion in the index.

The

The affigning adequate trivial names to the fhells, except in a few inftances, hath been omitted, through the fear of giving fuch as might any way inter-fere with thofe already given by Linnæus, to Shells of the fame kinds, the principal aim has been to give concife and accurate defcriptions of them ; how they may be approved, is fubmitted to the public.

As it is an allowed difficulty to determine where one clafs of Shells ends, and another begins, a liberty is taken of placing all the compreffed Snails under the title H E L I X , and thofe with a produced clavicle, whether lefs or more, and whether the aperture be. round or oval, or tending to either form, under the title T U R B O, which it is hoped will be pardoned by the Critics in Conchology.

It having been fuggefted that many of thefe Shells may prove to be the fry of fhells heretofore publifhed, great care hath been taken to obviate that idea, feveral fpecimens fufpected to be fuch, have therefore been laid afide for future invefigation.

The Author begs leave to inform his readers, that he will continue his refearches ; and if he fhould be fo fuccefsful as to procure a fufficient number of Shells for another plate, it fhall be publifhed feparately, as an appendix, to accommodate the prefent purchafers, without putting them again to the expence of the whole : And that he fhall think himfelf much obliged to any Gentleman who will favour him with any minute Shells here unnoticed, with an account where difcovered, or any other obfervations tending to illuftrate this part of our natural hiftory

FAVERSHAM,   GEO. WALKER.

E R R A T A.

Page 4. Fig. 15. read imperforato tranfverfe ftriatum.
      9.   31. read depictus.
      19.   68. read Subumbilicatus.
      22.   79. read arcis.
      24.   85. read ftriated.

The Defects in the Punctuation it is hoped will be excufed ; and the Date May 1, 1784, added at the End of the Introduction.

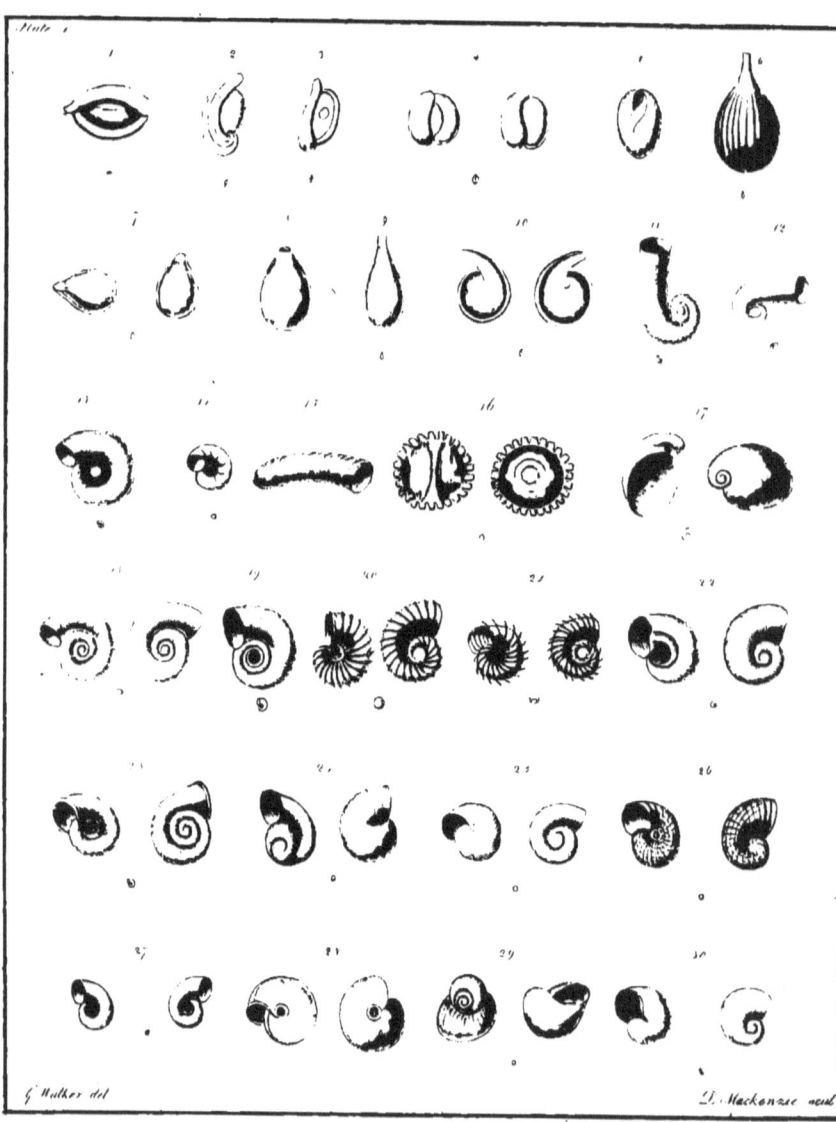

THE

EXPLANATORY INDEX

OF THE

Species of SHELLS contained in the Three Plates

WITH THE

Places where found, and their Degrees of Rarity.

SERPULA. The Wormshell.

FIG. 1.

SERPULA   Subovalis intorta umbilico pervio.

The hollow oval Wormshell,

The colour white and glossy,

It varies in size and shape, and is found in every portion of the sea sand which hath been examined.

An Linnæi S. N. p. 1264 — 791 Seminulum? Gualtieri Tab. 10. F. S.

FIG. 2.

SERPULA   Bicornis ventricosa.

The bellied semilunar Wormshell,

The colour white, opaque and glossy,

From Sandwich and Reculver—tho' not common.

FIG. 3.

F I G. 3.

SERPULA Bicornis umbilico perforato.

The femilunar perforated Wormfhell,
The colour white, opaque and gloffy,
From Sandwich—very rare.

F I G. 4.

SERPULA Subrotunda dorfo elevato.

The roundifh Wormfhell with an elevated back,
The colour white, opaque and gloffy,
In the fand of all the different parts of the fhore.

F I G. 5.

SERPULA Tenuis ovalis lœvis.

The thin fmooth egg-fhaped Wormfhell,
The colour pellucid, with milky veins,
From Sandwich—not common

F I G. 6.

SERPULA (Lagena) ftriata fulcata rotunda.

The round ftriated and furrowed Flafk Wormfhell,
The colour whitifh, tranfparent and gloffy,
From Sandwich, Reculver, and Shepey—very rare.

F I G. 7.

SERPULA (Lagena) marginata.

The bordered Flafk Wormfhell,
The colour white, tranfparent and gloffy,
From Reculver—very rare.

SERPULA (*Lagena*) lævis globofa.

The fmooth round Flafk Wormfhell,

The colour white and tranfparent,

From Sandwich—very rare.

F I G. 9.

SERPULA (*Lagena*) lævis ovalis.

The fmooth oval Flafk Wormfhell,

The colour bluifh-white, very tranfparent like glafs,

From Sandwich—very rare

F I G. 10.

SERPULA (*Retorta*) rotunda marginata cervice curvatim exerto.

The marginated Retort Wormfhell,

The colour white and opaque,

From Sandwich—not common.

F I G. 11.

SERPULA Recta anfractibus tribus contiguis regulariter involutis.

The ftrait horn Wormfhell, with three clofe intorted fpires at the tip,

The colour white, femitranfparent,

From Sandwich — rare.

This fhell, tho' refembling the femilituus of Linneus, p. 1163, N° 280, is not of the genus of Nautilus, having neither fyphon in the aperture, nor the internal concamerated ftructure.

B 2   F I G.

F I G. 12.

SERPULA   Recta umbilico pervio anfractu apicis unico involuto.

The fingle fpired ftrait horn Wormfhell with a pervious umbilicus,

The colour whitifh, tranfparent and gloffy,

From Reculver — very rare.

F I G. 13.

SERPULA   Quatuor anfractibus umbilicata apertura rotunda.

The four fpired round mouth umbilicated Wormfhell,

The colour white, opaque and gloffy,

From Sandwich — not common.

F I G. 14.

SERPULA   Apertura rotunda anfractibus duobus umbilicata.

The two-fpired umbilicated round mouth Wormfhell,

The colour white, opaque and glofiy,

Found adhering to lobfters, both fingle and in clufters.

D E N T A L E.   The Toothfhell.

F I G. 15.

DENTALE   Apice imperforata tranfverfaliter fubftriata.

The imperforated tranfverfly ftriated toothfhell,

The colour white and opaque,

From Sandwich — not very common.

PATELLA

PATELLA. The Limpet.

FIG. 16.

PATELLA   Plana orbiculata margine regulariter dentato.

> The toothed-wheel limpet,
> The colour white and opaque,
> From Sandwich — extreamly rare.

HELIX. The depreſſed Snail.

FIG. 17.

HELIX   Apertura patentiſlima.

> The very wide mouth ſnail,
> The colour white, tinged with pale red pellucid,
> From Sandwich and Reculver — very rare.

> It ſomewhat reſembles Mr. Pennant's Fig. 139, pl. 86, but is a ſea ſhell flatter, thick, and without tranſverſe wrinkles.

FIG. 18.

HELIX   Cornea quatuor anfractibus apertura rotunda.

> The horn ſnail of four ſpires with a round mouth.
> The colour of horn pellucid,
> In a freſh water Stream, near Faverſham.

FIG. 19.

HELIX   Umbilicata quatuor anfractibus apertura ſubrotunda.

> The umbilicated ſnail of four ſpires with a roundiſh mouth,
> The colour brown and opaque,
> From the ſame place as N° 18.

FIG. 21

F I G. 20.

H E L I X   Striata apertura compreſſa tribus anfraƈtibus carinata.

The ſtriated ſuboval mouth'd ſnail of three ſpires and a ſharp edge.

The colour light brown pellucid,

From the ſame place as Nº 18.

F I G. 21.

H E L I X   Subglobofa umbilicata ore ſubrotundo margine ſpinoſo.

The roundiſh mouth deeply umbilicated ſnail with a thorny margin,

The colour brown pellucid,

From Byſing Wood, near Faverſham — exceeding rare.

F I G. 22.

H E L I X   Umbilico profundo trium anfraƈtuum apertura ſubrotunda.

The ſnail with three ſpires, deep umbilicus, and a roundiſh mouth,

The colour white, opaque and gloſſy,

From Sandwich — not common.

F I G. 23.

H E L I X   Paludoſa compreſſa tribus anfraƈtibus ore rotundo reflexo.

The bog ſnail of three ſpires, with the border of the round mouth reflected,

The colour white and opaque,

In marſhy ground near Faverſham — common.

This elegant Shell is here engraved, as before, only deſcribed by Dacoſta from Morton's Northamptonſhire, p. 417.

F I G. 24.

H E L I X   Apertura ampla ovali anfractibus apicis refupinatis.

        The fnail with a large oval mouth, and the fpires of the tip turned
          backwards,   ·

.   The colour of horn femipellucid and glofly,

       From Sandwich — very rare.

F I G. 25.

H E L I X   Globofa duobus anfractibus lævis apertura fubrotunda.

       The fmooth round fnail with two fpires and a roundifh mouth,

       The colour white, opaque and glofly,

       From Sandwich — not common.

F I G. 26.

H E L I X   Unici anfractus fubumbilicata apertura rotunda marginata eleganter
         reticulata.

       The round mouth'd reticulated fingle fpired flightly fubumbilicated
         fnail,

       The colour white and pellucid,

       From Reculver — extreamly rare.

F I G 27.

H E L I X   Utrinque umbilicata apertura rotunda unici anfractus.

       The fingle fpired umbilicated round mouth'd fnail,

       The colour white, opaque and glofly,

       From Sandwich — not common.

F I G. 28.

F I G. 28

HELIX   Lineata dorfo convexo umbilicata margine acuto.

The lineated fnail with two central white lines croffing the umbilicus
and a fharp edged margin,

The colour chefnut and pellucid,

From Hernhill Brooks on Flags—very rare.

F I G. 29.

HELIX   Striata apertura fubovali anfractibus fupradorfalibus.

The oval mouth'd ftriated fnail with the fpires reflected on the back,

The colour greenifh — white pellucid,

From Sandwich — very rare.

F I G. 30.

HELIX   Anfractibus duobus apertura fubrotunda ad umbilicum conrctata.

The fnail with two fpires, and a roundifh aperture contracted near
the umbilicus,

The colour white and pellucid,

From Sandwich — not common.

T U R B O.

Plate II.

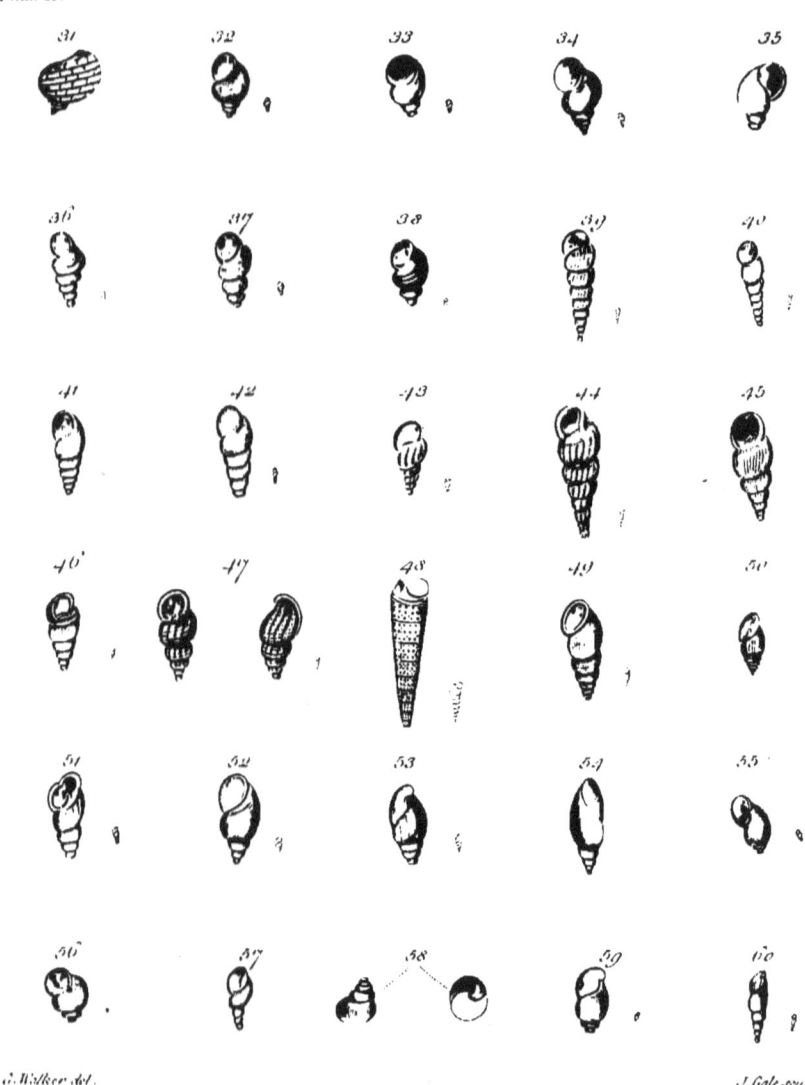

J. Walker del.

J. Cale scu

T U R B O.   The produced Snail.

P L A T E   II.

F I G. 31.

T U R B O Quinque anfractibus lævis cancellatim depictas.

The painted turbo with five fpires,

The colour white and brown elegantly checquered.

From Dover, by the Rev. Mr. Lyon — not uncommon.

An varietas Turbinis I'ttorei Lin. S. N. p. 1232, Nº 607.
The engraving is double the natural fize of the fhell.

F I G. 32.

T U R B O Subumbilicatus quatuor anfractibus reticulatis apertura fubrotunda.

The flightly umbilicated turbo with four reticulated fpires, and a roundifh aperture,

The colour white and pellucid.

From Seafalter — very rare.

F I G. 33.

T U R B O Lævis tribus anfractibus apertura rotunda.

The fmooth three fpired turbo with a round aperture,

The colour of horn pellucid,

From Faverfham Creek — not common.

F I G. 34.

F I G. 34.

T U R B O Lævis quinque anfractibus apertura fubrotunda marginata.
The fmooth five fpired turbo with a roundifh bordered aperture,
The colour whitifh and opaque,
From Sandwich—not uncommon.

F I G. 35.

T U R B O Lævis contrarius tribus anfractibus apertura fubrotunda.
The fmooth reverfed three fpired turbo with a roundifh aperture,
The colour white pellucid,
From Reculver—exceeding rare.

F I G. 36.

T U R B O Quinque anfractibus ventricofis apertura fubrotunda.
The five fpired ventricofe turbo with a roundifh mouth,
The colour white and opaque,
From Reculver—very rare.

F I G. 37.

T U R B O Tumidus quatuor anfractibus reticulatis apertura fubovali.
The turbo with four tumid reticulated fpires, with an oval aperture,
The colour white and opaque,
From Sandwich – very rare.

FIG. 38.

F I G. 38.

T U B B O   Tribus anfractibus primo ftrigis tribus tranfverfis apertura fubovata.

The three fpired turbo, the firft fpire with three tranfverfe ridges, and a fuboval aperture,

The colour opaque white,

From Seafalter—very rare.

F I G. 39.

T U R B O   Turritus novem anfractibus ftriatis apertura rotunda.

The taper turbo with nine ftriated fpires and a round aperture,

The colour white and opaque,

From Sandwich—very rare.

F I G. 40.

T U R B O   Turritus feptem anfractibus ftrigatis apertura ovali.

The taper turbo with feven ridged fpires and an oval aperture,

The colour opaque white,

From Sandwich—rare.

F I G. 41.

T U R B O   Sex anfractibus ftriatis apertura fubrotunda marginata.

The fix fpired ftriated turbo with a roundifh marginated aperture,

The colour opaque brown,

From a ditch-bank near Faverfham—not common.

F I G. 42.

T U R B O Quinque anfractibus striatis apertura subovali.

The five spired striated turbo with a suboval aperture,

The colour opaque brown,

From Byfing Wood, near Faverfham—very rare.

F I G. 43.

T U R B O Quinque anfractibus subcarinatis apice purpureo apertura ovali.

The five spired turbo, longitudinally and slightly ridged with an oval
  aperture,

The colour white with a purple tip.

From Sandwich, and Faverfham Creek—not uncommon.

F I G. 44.

T U R B O Turritus carinatus septem anfractibus apertura coarctata marginata.

The taper carinated turbo with seven spires and a contracted marginated aperture,

The colour opaque white.

From Sandwich—very rare.

F I G. 45.

T U R B O Clathratus sex anfractibus apertura ovali marginata.

The barred six spired turbo with an oval marginated aperture,

The colour opaque white.

From Sandwich— exceeding rare.

F I G. 24.

F I G. 46.

TURBO Longitudinaliter ſtriatus quinque anfractibus apertura ſubrotunda.
The ſtriated turbo with five ſpires and a roundiſh aperture,
The colour opaque white.
From Sandwich—not uncommon.

F I G. 47.

TURBO Craſſus clathratus quinque anfractibus apertura rotunda marginata.
The thick barred turbo of five ſpires and a round marginated aperture
The colour opaque white,
From Sandwich—very rare.

F I G. 48.

TURBO Turritus perverſus novem anfractibus punctatis apertura coarctata.
The reverſed taper turbo of nine dotted ſpires and ſtraitned aperture,
The colour light-brown opaque,
From Sandwich—not common.

F I G. 49.

TURBO Sex anfractibus reticulatis apertura ovali ſubmarginata.
The ſix ſpired reticulated turbo with an oval ſubmarginated aperture,
The colour ſemipellucid white,
From Shepey iſland—very rare.

F I G. 50

F I G. 50.

T U R B O Sex anfractibus apertura ovali bidentata.

The double toothed turbo of fix fpires and an oval aperture,

The colour opaque brown and glofly,

On the roots of rufhes in marfhes near Faverfham—very common.

F I G. 51.

T U R B O Striatus fex anfractibus apertura ovali bidentata marginata.

The ftriated double toothed marginated turbo of fix fpires and an oval aperture,

The colour femipellucid white.

In the mofly banks of a ftream near Faverfham—common.

F I G. 52.

T U R B O Quatuor anfractibus fubumbilicatus reticulatus apertura ovali.

The reticulated four fpired fubumbilicated turbo with an oval aperture

The colour pellucid white.

From Shepey ifland—very rare.

F I G. 53.

T U R B O Quatuor anfractibus apertura unidentata.

The four fpired turbo with a one toothed oval aperture,

The colour brown femipellucid glofly,

In mofs of boggy ground near Faverfham—not uncommon.

F I G. 54

F I G, 54.

T U R B O Stagnalis perverfus quinque anfractibus apertura ovali.

The reverfed lake turbo of five fpires and oval aperture,

The colour femipellucid brown and glofly,

On the bank of a ftream near Faverfham—not uncommon.

This feems defcribed by Petiver, tho' very indifferently engraved, Gaz. T. 10. f. 8.

F I G. 55.

T U R B O Tribus anfractibus reticulatis apertura unidentata.

The three fpired elegantly reticulated turbo with a one toothed oval aperture,

The colour pellucid white.

From Sandwich—exceeding rare.

F I G. 56

T U R B O Tribus anfractibus umbilicatus apertura fubrotunda.

The three fpired umbilicated turbo with a roundifh aperture,

The colour greenifh white pellucid,

From Faverfham Creek—not common.

F I G, 57.

T U R B O Striatus quatuor anfractibus apertura ovali marginata.

The ftriated four fpired turbo with an oval marginated aperture,

The colour opaque white,

From a ftream near Faverfham—very rare,

T R O C H U S.

TROCHUS. The Topshell.

FIG. 58.

TROCHUS Umbilicatus quinque anfractibus marginatus apertura subrotunda.

The five spired umbilicated marginated topshell with a roundish aperture,

The colour opaque brown,

From Sandwich — common.

BUCCINUM. The Whilk.

FIG. 59.

BUCCINUM Ampullaceum tribus anfractibus apertura ovali.

The bellied whilk of three spires with an oval aperture,

The colour opaque white,

From Faversham Creek—very rare.

FIG. 60.

BUCCINUM Turritum quinque anfractibus apertura ovali.

The taper whilk of five spires with an oval aperture,

The colour white, semipellucid and glossy,

In Faversham Creek only—but not uncommon there.

VOLUTA.

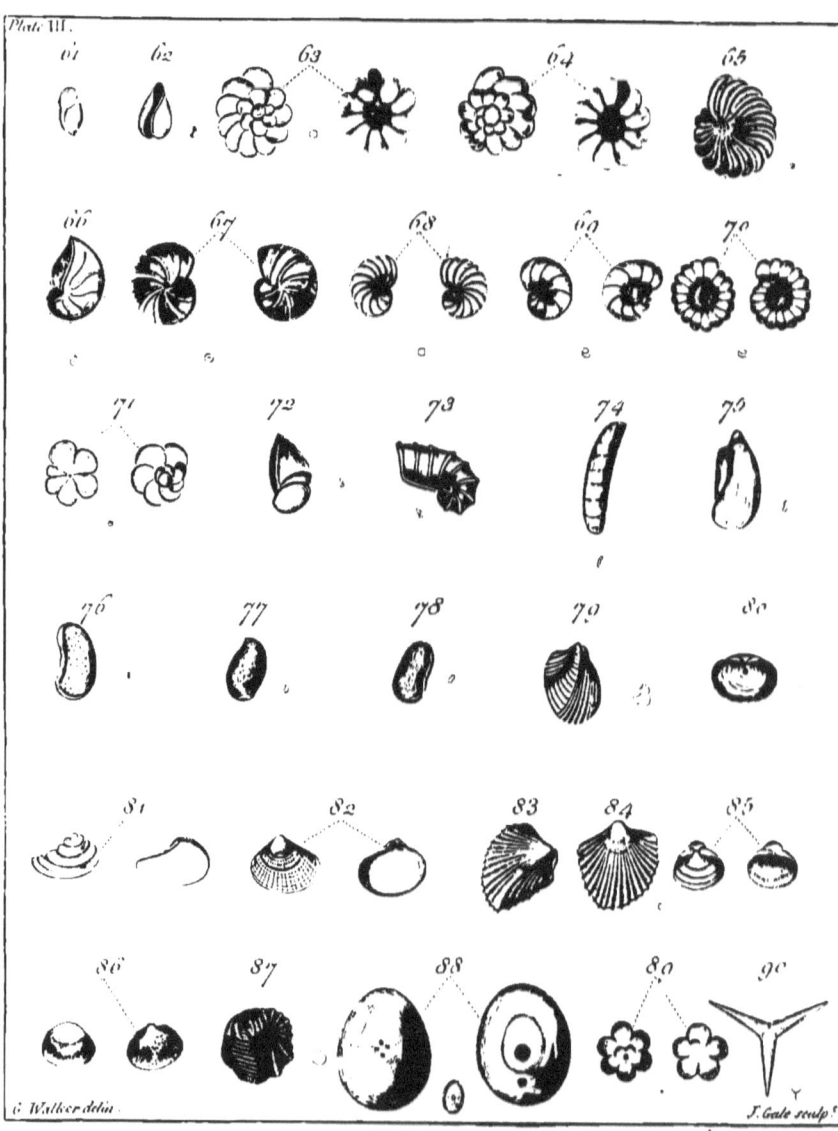

Plate III.

61 62 63 64 65

66 67 68 69 70

71 72 73 74 75

76 77 78 79 80

81 82 83 84 85

86 87 88 89 90

G. Walker delin.

J. Gale sculp.

V O L U T A. The Volute.

F I G. 61.

VOLUTA Alba opaca longitudinaliter ftriata.

The white opaque volute,

This fhell refembles Mr. Pennant's voluta jonenfis, but differs in the
form of the aperture, as well as in the fize.

From Sandwich and Shepey ifland — not uncommon.

B U L L A. The Dipper.

F I G. 62.

BULLA Craffa apertura medio coarctata.

The thick dipper, with a compreffed aperture,

The colour white and opaque.

From Reculver — very rare,

D

F I G. 63.

NAUTILUS. The Chambered Nautilus.

F I G. 63.

NAUTILUS Spiralis umbilicatus geniculis infculptis.

> The fpiral umbilicated nautilus with deep joints,

> The colour, while the fifh is alive, is a fine pellucid crimfon; when dead, is white.

> It is found alive on the fucus veficulofus, and is a very common fhell on all the coaft, and feems to be an univerfal littoral one, by the numbers found at Rimino, and in the fand of the South Seas.

> Lin. S. N. p. 1162, No. 276. Nautilus Beccarii.
> Planch. Tab. 1. Fig. 1. Gualtier, Tab. 19. Fig. H, H, I.

F I G. 64.

NAUTILUS Beccarii perverfus,

> The fpiral reverfed nautilus,

> This exactly refembles No 63, except being reverfed, and is not uncommonly found in the fame fand with it.

F I G. 65.

NAUTILUS Spiralis geniculis crenatis.

> The fpiral nautilus, with crenated joints,

> The colour opaque white.

> The fineft fpecimens are from Shepey — not uncommon.

> Lin. S. N. p. 1162, No. 275, crifpus. Planch T. 1. f. 2. Gualt T. 19. f. A. D.

F I G. 66.

F I G. 66.

NAUTILUS Spiralis apertura lineari geniculis elevatis.

The fpiral nautilus, with a narrow aperture and raifed joints,

The colour opaque white.

From Shepey ifland — not common.

Lin. S. N. 1162, No. 274, calcar.   Pl. T. 1. f. 3, 4.   Gualt T. 19. f. C. B.

F I G. 67.

NAUTILUS Spiralis geniculis lævibus.

The fpiral nautilus with fmooth joints,

The colour femipellucid, white and glofly.

From Sandwich and Seafalter — not common.

F I G. 68.

NAUTILUS Spiralis utrinque fubumbilicatas geniculis depreffis plurimis.

The fpiral fubumbilicated nautilus, with many depreffed joints,

The colour opaque white.

From Reculver — very rare.

F I G. 69.

NAUTILUS Spiralis umbilicatus geniculis fulcatis.

The umbilicated fpiral nautilus, with furrowed joints.

The colour opaque white.

From Sandwich — not common.

F I G. 70.

F I G. 70.

NAUTILUS Spiralis craffus utrinque umbilicatus geniculis lineatis.

> The thick fpiral doubly umbilicated nautilus, with fine joints,
> The colour opaque white.
> From Reculver — exceeding rare.

F I G. 71.

NAUTILUS Spiralis lobatus anfractibus fupra rotundatis fubtus depreffioribus.

> The fpiral lobated nautilus, with the fpires rounded on the upper
> fide, and depreffed on the under.
> Colour opaque white.
> From Whitftable — not common.

F I G. 72.

NAUTILUS Oblongus carinatus apertura lineari ovali.

> The oblong carinated nautilus, with a narrow oval aperture,
> The colour whitifh, tranfparent like glafs.
> From Seafalter and Sandwich — very rare.

F I G. 73.

NAUTILUS Subarcuatus geniculis exertis.

> The bending nautilus with raifed joints,
> The colour opaque brown.
> From Shepey ifland — very rare.

FIG. 74.

NAUTILUS Rectus geniculis depreffis.

The ftrait nautilus with depreffed joints,

The colour pellucid white.

From Sandwich — exceeding rare.

M Y T I L U S.   The Mufcle.

FIG. 75.

MYTILUS Striatus umbonibus productis.

The ftriated mufcle with lengthened beaks,.

The colour pellucid white.

From Reculver and Sandwich — not uncommon.

FIG. 76.

MYTILUS Lævis valvulis antice inflexis.

The fmooth mufcle, with the valves inflected in front,

The colour brown and glofly.

From a frefh water ftream near Faverfham — common.

FIG. 77.

MYTILUS Subrhombiformis punctatus.

The fubrombic dotted mufcle,

The colour pellucid white.

From Sandwich — common.

F I G 78.

MYTILUS Subovalis denfiffime punctatus.

The fuboval thickly dotted mufcle,

The colour pellucid white.

From Sandwich — not uncommon.

F I G. 79.

MYTILUS Difcors arcis tribus diftinctis.

The divided mufcle,

The colour opaque brown,

From Sandwich — not common.

Lin. S. N. 1159, No. 261. Da Cofta Fr. Conch. p. 221. Tab. 17. f. 1. where it is exactly defcribed, and as badly engraved.

A N O M I A. The Scale.

F I G. 80.

A N O M I A Squammula.

The fcale anomia,

The colour opaque white and glofly.

From Sandwich — not uncommon.

Lin. S. N. 1151, No. 221.

This fhell is well defcribed by Da Cofta; but neither he or Mr. Pennant have caufed it to be engraved.

A R C A.

A R C A.   The Ark.

F I G. 81.

ARCA Oblonga ftriata antice angulata.

The oblong ftriated ark, with the forefide angulated,

The colour opaque white.

From Sandwich — not uncommon.

Lin. S. N. p. 1141, No. 171. Arca Modiolus.

C A R D I U M.   The Cockle.

F I G. 82.

CARDIUM Striatum radiatum.

The ftriated and radiated cockle,

The colour opaque white.

From Sandwich — common.

This feems to refemble the cardium edule, Lin. S. N. p. 1124, No. 90; but on com-parifon will be found to differ from it.

F I G. 83.

CARDIUM Subcordatum fubangulatum.

The truncated heart cockle,

The colour opaque white.

From Seafalter — very rare.

Lin. S. N. p. 1123, No. 83.

Dr Lifter's H. C. Tab. 317, No. 154, fomewhat refembles this fhell, but is not tranfverfely ftriated.

F I G. 84.

F I G. 84.

CARDIUM Subcordatum antice muricatum.

The heart cockle, with the front muricated,

The colour opaque white.

From Shepey ifland — not uncommon.

F I G. 85.

CARDIUM Striatum apicibus reflexis.

The fmooth cockle with reflected beaks,

The colour opaque brown.

From Sandwich — not common.

F I G. 86.

CARDIUM Læve apice minuto.

The fmooth fmall beaked cockle,

The colour femipellucid, pale red and glofly.

From Shepey ifland — rare.

The title of cardium to this and the precedent is doubtfully given.

L E P A S. The Acorn Shell.

F I G. 87.

L E P A S Balanus ftriatus apertura obliqua.

The ftriated acorn fhell, with an oblique aperture,

The colour light brown.

From Sandwich, on the roots of fea-weeds; the fineft fpecimens on lobfters — not uncommon.

APPENDIX.

A P P E N D I X.

•

E C H I N U S. The Sea Urchin.

F I G. 88.

ECHINUS Ovalis depreſſus ambulacris quinis.

The five rayed depreſſed oval ſea urchin,

The colour opaque white.

From Sandwich — common.

This is nearly allied to Lin. p. 1104, No. 14 ; but wants the five lines on the under ſide.

F I G. 89.

ECHINUS Subrotundus planus lobatus.

The flat roundiſh lobated echinus,

The colour opaque white.

From Reculver — rare.

A S T E R I A S. The Star Fiſh.

F I G. 90.

ASTERIAS Triradiata lævis.

The ſmooth three rayed ſtarfiſh,

The colour white, tranſparent as glaſs,

On all the different ſhores that have been examined.

www.ingramcontent.com/pod-product-compliance
Lightning Source LLC
Chambersburg PA
CBHW030912260626
47169CB00008B/2817